Disney's Beauty AND THE Beast

• THE ENCHANTED CHRISTMAS •

GROLIER BOOKS

It was a very special Christmas. Everyone in the castle was happy now that the prince and beautiful Belle were so much in love. The cook, Mrs. Potts, and her little son, Chip, and old Cogsworth, the head butler, joined Belle and the prince, and they all watched as sweet young Angelique and jolly Lumiere finished decorating the tree.

Little Chip thought that the castle looked beautiful now. As Belle and the prince left the room, he asked his mother, "Was it just as beautiful last year, Mother? I can't remember!"

Mrs. Potts took her son on her lap and said,
"Well, Chip, last year was very different. At first
we weren't sure there would even be a Christmas!"

"But I got our master and Belle together. I saved
Christmas!" cried tall, thin Lumiere.

"No, I did it!" said short, fat Cogsworth.

"Well," said Mrs. Potts, "I think we all helped. You must remember that the Master was still a Beast, and we all looked completely different because of that dreadful magic spell. But Belle seemed rather to like the Master, even though he was so dreadfully bad tempered!

…And so, just before Christmas, we encouraged him to take her out ice skating!"

But the Beast wasn't used to being with pretty young ladies. He felt rather shy and embarrassed. And he certainly didn't want to slip and fall on the ice. Not in front of Belle!

But soon, with Belle's help and encouragement,
the Beast learned to move along the ice next to
her. At first he was a little shaky, but gradually he
began to enjoy himself.

Meanwhile, high up in the castle, a little piccolo called Fife looked down and watched them. "Quick! Tell me. What do you see?" bellowed Forte, the great organ on the wall behind him. You see, before the magic spell was put on the castle, Fife had been a piccolo player, and Forte had been the castle's court composer.

When Fife told Forte that the Beast was skating with a pretty young girl, Forte was jealous. He became furious. "The Master should be listening to my music and not wasting time with young girls!" he bellowed. Then he sent little Fife out to spy on Belle and the Beast.

Outside, little Fife found Belle lying on her back in the snow, moving her arms and legs to make a "snow angel". Of course the Beast wanted to make his own snow angel, too.

But when the Beast saw the pattern he had made
in the snow, he became very angry with himself.

"Look at me," he growled. "I'm so ugly I can't
even make angels in the snow. I just leave
monsters behind me!"

Then he hurried back to the castle. His good
mood was ruined.

Belle felt so sorry for the Beast
that she decided that she would give
him a very special Christmas present. But what?
When she got back to the castle she had an idea. Belle
sat down and began to write a story for the Beast. A story
that might give him hope!

Meanwhile down in the kitchen all the servants were talking about Christmas. But not Cogsworth. The little clock said, "There will be no Christmas this year. No Christmas! Don't you remember? It was at Christmas time that the Master was changed into a Beast and we were all changed, too!"

"No Christmas? What a shame!" said Mrs. Potts with a smile. "That will mean no roast turkey, no lovely pudding, no sweet, delicious Christmas cake."

"Christmas cake?" said Cogsworth, his mouth suddenly watering. "Well, I suppose we could have a little Christmas celebration…with Christmas cake and turkey!" he said.

Later, Belle joined the servants, and together they brought the Christmas decorations down from the attic. But one of the decorations, a little angel named Angelique, was sceptical. "Our master, the Beast, will never let us hold a real Christmas. The memory of Christmas is still too painful for him!" she reminded them.

But the whole time that Belle and the others were decorating, little Fife was watching their every move.

"I must tell Forte everything I've seen!" he said to himself. "He certainly won't be pleased about this!"

When Fife told the great organ about Belle's Christmas plans, Forte laughed and said, "Ha, now I know how we can get our master away from that foolish young girl!"

And, when the Beast came up to hear some music, Forte told him all about the Christmas decorations!

The Beast exploded with anger at the mere mention of Christmas! For, not long ago, he had still been a rich and handsome young prince—who was unfortunately both selfish and vain. And it had been at Christmas time that an old woman had come to his door and asked for shelter…

…and when the selfish young prince unkindly told her to go away, she turned herself into a good fairy. And she changed the prince into a Beast as a punishment!

"You and everyone in your castle will only turn back to normal if you can get a young girl to love a Beast like you!" she had told the shocked prince.

So naturally the Beast hated Christmas and everything connected with it.

After hearing about Belle's Christmas plans from Forte, the Beast searched the castle for Belle. Eventually he found her in the cellar, choosing a yule log for the Christmas fire.

"There will be no Christmas. Now or ever again!" he bellowed, and took the yule log from her.

But when they got upstairs Belle brought out the story she had written and gave it to the Beast.

"Well, if there is to be no Christmas," she said to him with a smile, "then I had better give you your present now!"

The Beast felt guilty for bellowing at Belle, and even worse because he had no Christmas present for her. So he rushed upstairs and commanded Forte to compose a happy Christmas tune in Belle's honour!

Forte didn't like that command at all!

Meanwhile, Belle and little Chip were outside
in the castle grounds, looking for a suitable Christmas
tree. "We'll have Christmas whether the Beast likes
it or not!" she told Chip.

But all Belle and Chip could find were small,
bare trees!

Later, back in the castle, Belle was amazed to see the little footstool that had once been a dog, rushing upstairs. And so, curious, Belle followed. But Belle didn't know that Forte, the great organ, had ordered Fife to whistle loudly so the footstool would come…and so that Belle would follow!

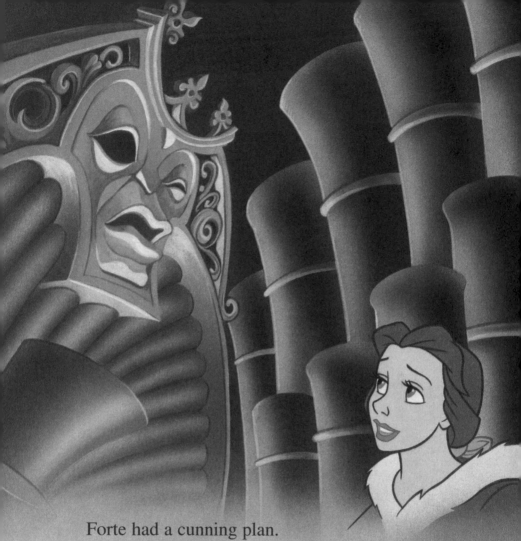

Forte had a cunning plan.
If he could convince the Beast
that Belle really hated him and was
looking for a chance to get away, then the Beast
would forget all about her and return to his only
love…Forte's organ music!

So Forte pretended to be nice. He lied and told
Belle that if she really wanted to please the Beast,
she should look for a wonderful Christmas tree far
out in the Black Forest!

After Belle and Chip had left the castle in search
of the perfect tree, the Beast tried to find Belle.
He wanted her to hear the tune that Forte had been
ordered to compose for her. But of course he
couldn't find her anywhere.

"Search for Belle everywhere!" the Beast told
Cogsworth.

But when Cogsworth and the others had searched everywhere without finding Belle, the Beast looked into his magic mirror. And the mirror showed him that Belle was riding away from his castle.

The Beast, convinced that Belle was leaving
him, sadly climbed the stairs to the music room.
Heartbroken, he wished only to forget about Belle.

Forte pretended to be sympathetic. "I knew that
wretched girl never really cared for you. You
belong here with me and my wonderful music!"
the treacherous organ told the Beast.

But Forte's thundering music only made the Beast feel angrier. "I was a fool!" he bellowed. "I thought she liked me!"

And the Beast rushed downstairs in a rage, hurling plates and furniture across the room!

Meanwhile, far out in the Black Forest, Belle
had crossed the frozen lake and found the most
beautiful tree of all!

"Wait until your master sees this tree," she told
Chip with a smile. "He'll be ever so happy!"

But, on the way back
to the castle, the weight
of the tree made the horse
and cart crack the ice!

The terrified little Chip fell into the lake…

…and Belle plunged bravely into the icy water to save the little cup! Fife, who had been spying on them, was terrified!

Belle quickly swam to the bottom of the lake and she brought the little cup up to safety. But she couldn't pull herself out of the icy cold water!

In his magic mirror the Beast had seen Belle in the Black Forest, and was following her.

The Beast arrived just in time to see Belle go under. He jumped into the icy water to save her.

The Beast saved Belle from drowning, but he had not forgiven her! He still thought she had tried to escape from him, and that she had never really liked him.

So when they arrived back at the castle, he locked the unhappy Belle in the castle's dungeon to teach her a lesson!

But later, when the Beast was upstairs, he read Belle's story. It was the story of a good-hearted but misunderstood prince. But a prince with hope! And the Beast knew that Belle had been writing about him. At last he believed that Belle did like him.

The Beast hurried to the dungeon and brought Belle out. "Can you ever forgive me?" he asked her.

When Forte heard that Belle and the Beast were friends once more, the mighty organ went mad with rage, blasting out great explosions of sound. The music was so strong and violent that it cracked the walls and ceilings! The jealous Forte was trying his best to destroy Belle and everyone else in the castle!

The Beast bravely fought his way through the huge crashing timbers and the falling walls, until he reached the organ. Then he quickly smashed Forte's keyboard so that the villain had to stop making his awful noise. Forte was beaten!

"And what started out as the worst of Christmases, ended up as one of the very finest! Belle and the Master became the best of friends, and eventually that awful spell was broken!" said Mrs. Potts as she finished her story.

Yes, the Beast was now a handsome prince again. But when he had still been a hideous beast, Belle had given him the greatest gift of all: the gift of hope.

What an enchanted Christmas it had been!